LITTLE
GIANTS

BLUE TORTOISE

ALAN ROGERS

For a free color catalog describing Gareth Stevens' list of high-quality children's books, call 1-800-341-3569 (USA) or 1-800-461-9120 (Canada).

Library of Congress Cataloging-in-Publication Data
Rogers, Alan, 1952-
    Blue tortoise / Alan Rogers.
      p. cm. -- (Little giants)
    Summary: Although not as fast as the blue ant,
tiger, and rabbit, Blue Tortoise arrives first at the picnic.
    ISBN 0-8368-0404-X
    [1. Turtles--Fiction. 2. Animals--Fiction. 3. Blue--
Fiction. 4. Picnicking--Fiction.] I. Title. II. Series:
Rogers, Alan, 1952- Little giants.
PZ7.R62555B1 1990
[E]--dc20   90-9833

This North American edition first published in 1990 by
Gareth Stevens Children's Books
1555 North RiverCenter Drive, Suite 201
Milwaukee, Wisconsin 53212, USA

Printed in the United States of America

4 5 6 7 8 9 96 95 94

Gareth Stevens Children's Books
MILWAUKEE

Blue Tortoise is going to a picnic.

Everyone will be there.

"Wait for me!" says Blue Tortoise . . .

but Blue Rabbit hurries on to the picnic.

"Wait for me!" says Blue Tortoise . . .

but Blue Tiger hurries on to the picnic.

"Wait for me!" says Blue Tortoise . . .

but Blue Giraffe hurries on to the picnic.

"Wait for me!" says Blue Tortoise . . .

but the Blue Ants hurry on to the picnic.

"We're waiting for the boat," say
the others . . .

but Blue Tortoise walks slowly on
to the picnic.

"Wait for us!" they all shout . . .

but guess who gets there first!

SLURP!